THIS CANDLEWICK BOOK BELONGS TO:

_____

_____

_____

_____

To Carly, Olivia, and Jacob

First U.S. edition 1998

Library of Congress Cataloging-in-Publication Data

Postgate, Daniel.
Captain Hog : mission to the stars / Daniel Postgate. — 1st U.S. ed.
p.   cm.
Summary: Captain Hog and his animal crew search for the perfect
planet on which to build their new headquarters.
ISBN 0-7636-0410-0
[1. Domestic animals — Fiction. 2. Science fiction.] I. Title.
PZ7.P8387Cap   1998
[E] — dc21   97-7302

2 4 6 8 10 9 7 5 3 1

Printed in Hong Kong

This book was typeset in ITC Highlander.
The pictures were done in watercolor and pencil.

Candlewick Press
2067 Massachusetts Avenue
Cambridge, Massachusetts 02140

CAPTAIN HOG
MISSION TO THE STARS

DANIEL POSTGATE

CANDLEWICK PRESS
CAMBRIDGE, MASSACHUSETTS

Captain Hog and Officers Horse, Cow, Sheep, Chicken, and Mole were on their way back from a trip to the moon when they received a message on the Intergalactic Videophone.
"Earth to Captain Hog! Come in, Captain Hog. . . ."

It was Admiral Goat.
"I have a special mission for you," he said.
"Go and find us the perfect planet to build
our new headquarters on."

"Aye, aye, Sir!" said Captain Hog.
And off they flew, deep into
the universe.

Soon a planet came into view and they all beamed down to take a look.

"Oh no," said Captain Hog,
"this planet is far too small for us."

The second planet they visited already had creatures living on it—creatures who ate nothing but smelly cheese and never brushed their teeth or bathed.

"Welcome, earthlings," they said.
"Pooh!" said Captain Hog. "We'd love to stay
and talk to you, but you're far too smelly."

The next planet had candy growing
all over it!
"Yum, yum!" cried the crew.

"Back to the ship, everyone," ordered Captain Hog. "Too many sweets are bad for you."

Another planet was like a great big balloon.
"This planet won't do," said Captain Hog.
"It's much too bouncy."

There was even a planet made of pink pudding—Captain Hog and his crew fell straight through it and out the other side!

At last they found a planet they all liked very much. It was covered in lovely thick fur. "Mmmm, this is nice," said Captain Hog. "Perfect for a little snooze. . . ."

But it wasn't a planet
at all. It was a giant space
monster, and it found the crew
members far too itchy to let them stay.
"This is getting silly!"
said Captain Hog.

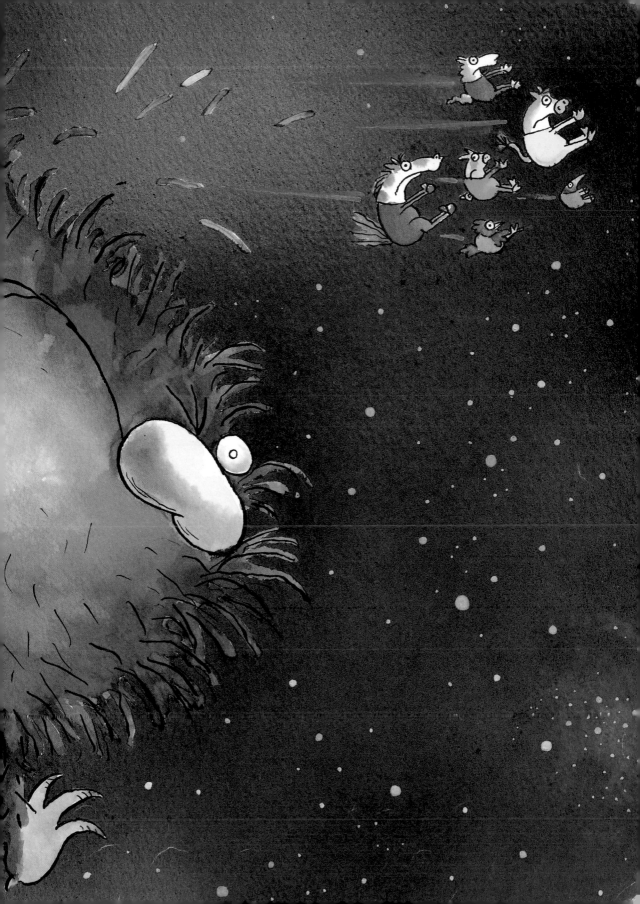

Captain Hog and his crew flew
all around the universe,
but none of the planets
they discovered seemed
quite right.

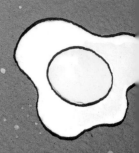

Finally they spotted a small
blue-green planet.
"Let's go there," said Captain Hog.

On that planet there were lots of fields
for Officer Horse to gallop around on . . .
lots of grass for Officer Cow and
Officer Sheep to eat . . .

lots of earth for Officer Mole to dig in . . .
and lots of bushes for Officer Chicken
to sit in. . . .
It was a perfect planet!

"CAPTAIN HOG!" boomed the voice of Admiral Goat.
"WHAT'S GOING ON?"

Captain Hog fumbled for his radio.
"I can hear you loud and clear, Sir!" he said.
"OF COURSE YOU CAN! I'M STANDING RIGHT BEHIND YOU."
That startled Captain Hog. "I thought you were
back home on planet Earth, Sir!" he said.
"This *is* planet Earth," sighed the Admiral.
"Oops," said Captain Hog.

"So, did you discover
a new planet for our
headquarters?" asked
Admiral Goat.
"No, Sir," said Captain
Hog. "But we discovered
something much more
important . . ."

"that there's n

place like home!"